RYAN'S DINOSAUR EGG-VENTURE!

story by Ryan Kaji and Mommy

SIMON SPOTLIGHT

An imprint of Simon & Schuster Children's Publishing Division • New York London Toronto Sydney New Delhi

1230 Avenue of the Americas, New York, New York 10020 • This Simon Spotlight edition January 2021

For more information about special discounts for bulk purchases, please contact Simon & Schuster Special Sales at 1-866-506-1949 or business@simonandschuster.com.

Manufactured in the United States of America 1020 LAK

2 4 6 8 10 9 7 5 3 1

ISBN 978-1-5344-8200-5 • ISBN 978-1-5344-8201-2 (eBook)

pocket.watch

RYAN'S WORLD

DINO UNIVERSE

Hi! I'm Ryan, and I'm exploring a dinosaur site with Alpha Lexa, Gus the Gummy Gator, and Combo Panda. Shelldon, Combo Panda's pet dinosaur, is also joining us.

Do you like dinosaurs? I think they're so cool. My favorite kind of dinosaur is the

T. rex.

What is your favorite dinosaur?

The site has a lot of dinosaur fossils, which are the remains of dinosaurs left behind in rocks. There are all kinds of fossils, like footprints, bones, and teeth. The scientists that look for fossils are called paleontologists.

You can find dinosaur fossils on every continent on Earth, and some of the fossils are almost 245 million years old. That's really, really old!

Look! What's this over here? These aren't fossils. . . . they are three mysterious eggs! What could be inside?
They must be dinosaur eggs with baby dinosaurs inside. Alpha awesome!
Don't even think about touching the eggs. What if there are monsters inside?
Monsters?!

What do you think? Should we hatch the eggs?

Let's hatch the eggs!

But what can we do to help?

Let's put our ears close to the eggs and listen.

Shhh!

Can you hear anything?

I can hear a tapping sound coming from inside. We should try tapping back with our fingers. Maybe just one tiny tap for each egg. Go on, give it a try!

The eggs didn't hatch, but they turned different colors: green, yellow, and blue. Which one is your favorite? I knew that dinosaur eggs came in different colors, like light blue and green, but I never knew they could change colors. That's strange!

We should show the baby dinosaurs that we are their friends, not their enemies. Let's do a super silly dinosaur roar and a super silly dinosaur dance!

Look, the eggs are beginning to tremble. Do you think they're nervous about hatching? I know what always makes me feel better when I'm nervous: a big hug!

Pick up the book and give it a

nice big squeeze!

I wonder if warming up the eggs will help them hatch. We could wrap them up in blankets, and we could make sure they get plenty of sunshine.

Pick up the book

and raise it high above your head, so it's as close to the sun as it can be. It's important for baby dinosaurs to stay warm!

Or baby monsters!

Whoa! That totally did not work at all. Now all the eggs are giant! Maybe that means the baby dinosaurs inside are still growing. They could be giant baby dinosaurs.

Or giant baby monsters!

The size of a dinosaur egg depends on the kind of dinosaur it is. It can be from one to **eighteen** inches long!

Oh wow! The eggs are beginning to crack. Let's help them along by clapping with our hands. *Clap, clap!*

I can't bear to watch!

The cracks are getting larger. If we clap faster, maybe the eggs will hatch faster too. Clap as fast as you can!

CLAP!
CLAP!
CLAP!

The eggs are now fully hatched!
Three baby dinosaurs have popped out of the eggs.
We're so EGG-CITED!

They were dinosaur eggs, not monster eggs!

Phew! I'm so relieved!

Let's get to know our new friends.

I'm a **Stegosaurus.** I have a lot of bony plates on my back, but I'm missing my set of front teeth. Instead, I use my beak and my back teeth to munch on plants.

I'm a **Triceratops.** Once I'm fully grown, the three horns on my head might be 45 inches long. That's about three times longer than a bowling pin!

I'm a
Pteranodon.
I'm not actually a dinosaur, but I'm closely related. I spend most of my day soaring over the ocean and looking for fish to eat. Yum!

Shelldon is so happy to have new friends to play with.
I'm excited too!
Thanks for helping us hatch the three mystery eggs. This has been a fun dinosaur egg-venture. I hope I see you again soon!